PEANUTS

It's the GREAT PUMPKIN, Charlie Brown™

ILLUSTRATED BY CHARLES M. SCHULZ CREATIVE ASSOCIATES

 phoenix international publications, inc.

SNOOPY HELPS CHARLIE BROWN CLEAN UP THE YARD. "THANKS, OLD PAL," SAYS CHARLIE BROWN. LOOK AROUND FOR THESE AUTUMN LEAVES.

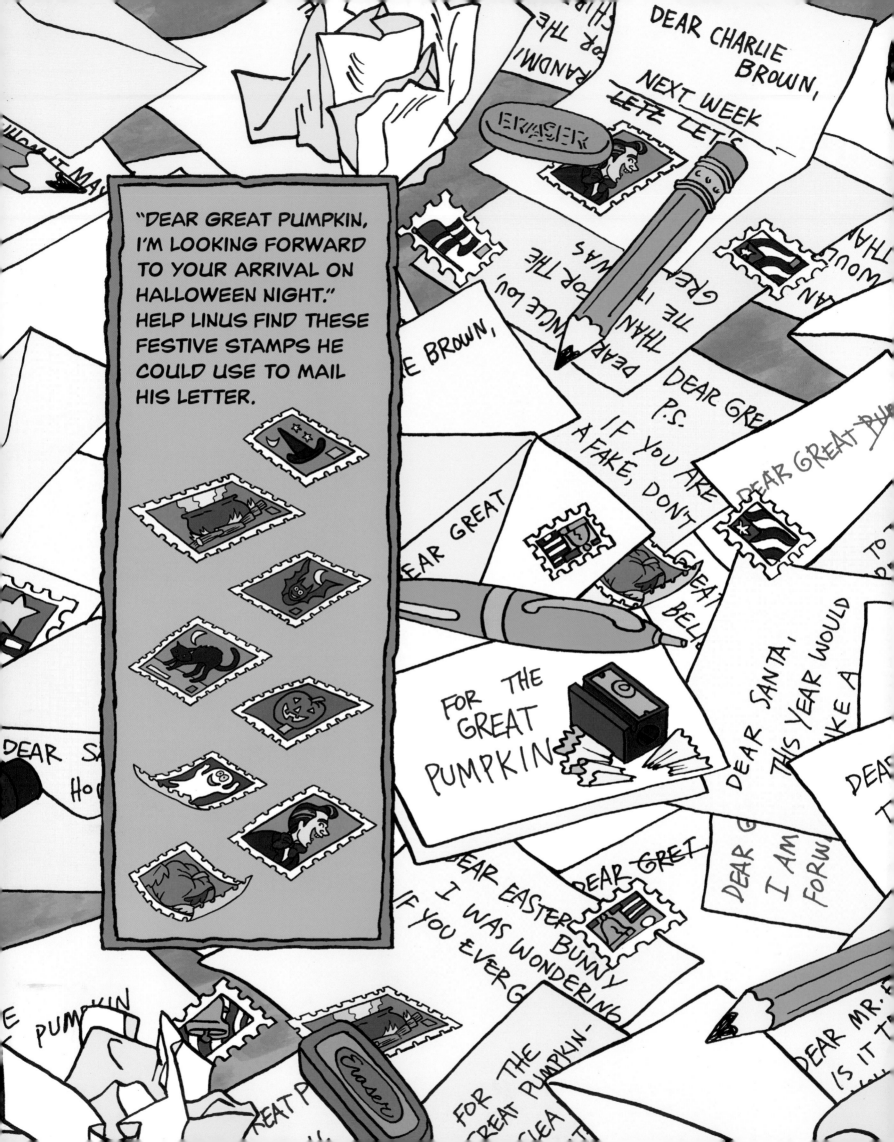

TRICK OR TREAT! LOOK AROUND THE NEIGHBORHOOD FOR THESE KIDS WHO ARE HOPING FOR SOMETHING GOOD TO EAT.

WHILE LINUS AND SALLY SAT IN THE PUMPKIN PATCH, THEIR FRIENDS GOT LOTS OF TREATS. LOOK THROUGH THE COLLECTION TO FIND THESE SWEETS.

THIS PIECE OF CANDY

THIS CANDY APPLE

THIS PIECE OF BUBBLE GUM

THIS POPCORN BALL

THIS CANDY BAR

THIS PIECE OF CANDY

THIS COOKIE

THIS YEAR, CHARLIE BROWN FINALLY GOT INVITED TO THE HALLOWEEN PARTY! SEARCH THE FESTIVE DECORATIONS FOR THESE PAPER CUTOUTS.

THIS GHOST

THIS MOON

THIS WITCH

THIS SKELETON

THIS BLACK CAT

THIS JACK-O-LANTERN

RETURN TO THE FALLING LEAVES TO FIND THESE LOST THINGS.

LINUS'S LOLLIPOP

SNOOPY'S BOWL

CHARLIE BROWN'S PARTY INVITATION

LUCY'S FOOTBALL

LINUS'S BLANKIE

LUCY'S MAGAZINE

GO BACK TO LINUS'S LETTERS TO THE GREAT PUMPKIN AND FIND SOME THAT DON'T BELONG.

DEAR AUNT MARIE,
DEAR UNCLE LOU,
DEAR SANTA,
DEAR CONGRESSMAN,
DEAR EASTER BUNNY,
DEAR SALLY,

ROLL BACK TO THE PUMPKIN PATCH TO FIND FESTIVE CLOUD SHAPES.

PRESIDENTS' DAY

INDEPENDENCE DAY

THANKSGIVING

NEW YEAR'S DAY

ST. PATRICK'S DAY

VALENTINE'S DAY

EARTH DAY

TROT BACK TO THE TRICK-OR-TREAT SCENE TO FIND THESE PIECES OF HALLOWEEN COSTUMES.

FLY BACK TO THE NIGHT
SKY TO FIND THESE
SHAPES IN THE STARS.

CHARLIE BROWN
WOODSTOCK
SNOOPY'S DOGHOUSE
SNOOPY
SCHROEDER'S PIANO
A FOOTBALL
SNOOPY'S BOWL
CHARLIE BROWN'S SHIRT

WHEN CHARLIE BROWN
WENT TRICK-OR-TREATING,
HE ONLY GOT ROCKS.
GO BACK TO THE TREATS
TO FIND THESE TRICKS.

RETURN TO THE FRENCH
COUNTRYSIDE TO FIND
THESE FARM TOOLS.

BOOGIE BACK TO THE
HALLOWEEN PARTY TO FIND
THESE JACK-O-LANTERNS.